Harry Potter

AND THE COBLET OF FIRE™

BOOK OF CREATURES
Create and Trace

SCHOLASTIC INC.

New York   Toronto   London   Auckland   Sydney
Mexico City   New Delhi   Hong Kong   Buenos Aires

ISBN 0-439-63296-X
Copyright © 2005 Warner Bros. Entertainment Inc.
HARRY POTTER and all related characters and elements are trademarks of and © Warner Bros. Entertainment Inc.
Harry Potter Publishing Rights © J.K. Rowling.
(s05)

Published by Scholastic Inc. SCHOLASTIC and associated logos are trademarks and/or registered trademarks of Scholastic Inc.

12 11 10 9 8 7 6 5 4 3 2 1   5 6 7 8 9/0

Designed by Two Red Shoes Design
Printed in the U.S.A.

First printing, November 2005

HARRY POTTER

CROOKSHANKS

ERROLL

SCABBERS

HEDWIG

DOBBY

FAWKES

GRIM

FANG

NORBERT

PIXIE

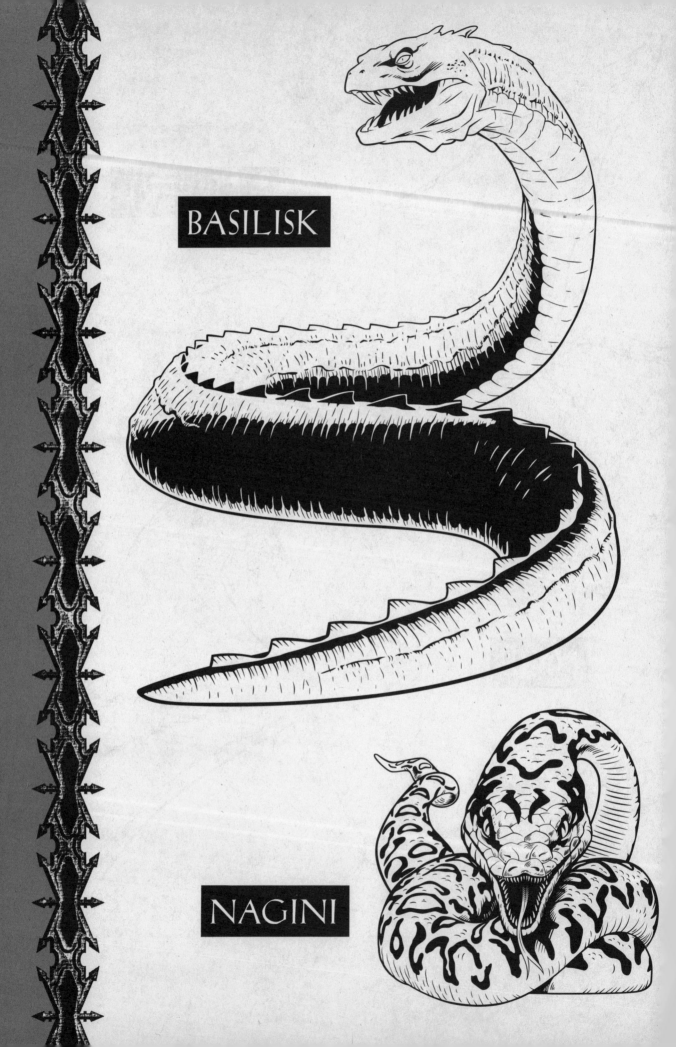

BASILISK

NAGINI